THIS BOOK BELONGS TO

....

Published in 2014 by Flying Books Ltd

ISBN 978-0-473-29546-2

Illustration and design: Cheryl Smith, www.macarndesign.com

For more Pee Wee the Kiwi adventures, go to www.peeweethekiwi.co.nz

Printed in China through Asia Pacific Offset Ltd

PEE WEE
THE LONELY KIWI
finds a new friend

BLAIR COOPER
ILLUSTRATED BY CHERYL SMITH

Pee Wee was a lonely kiwi,

so one day he went for a walk

to find a new friend.

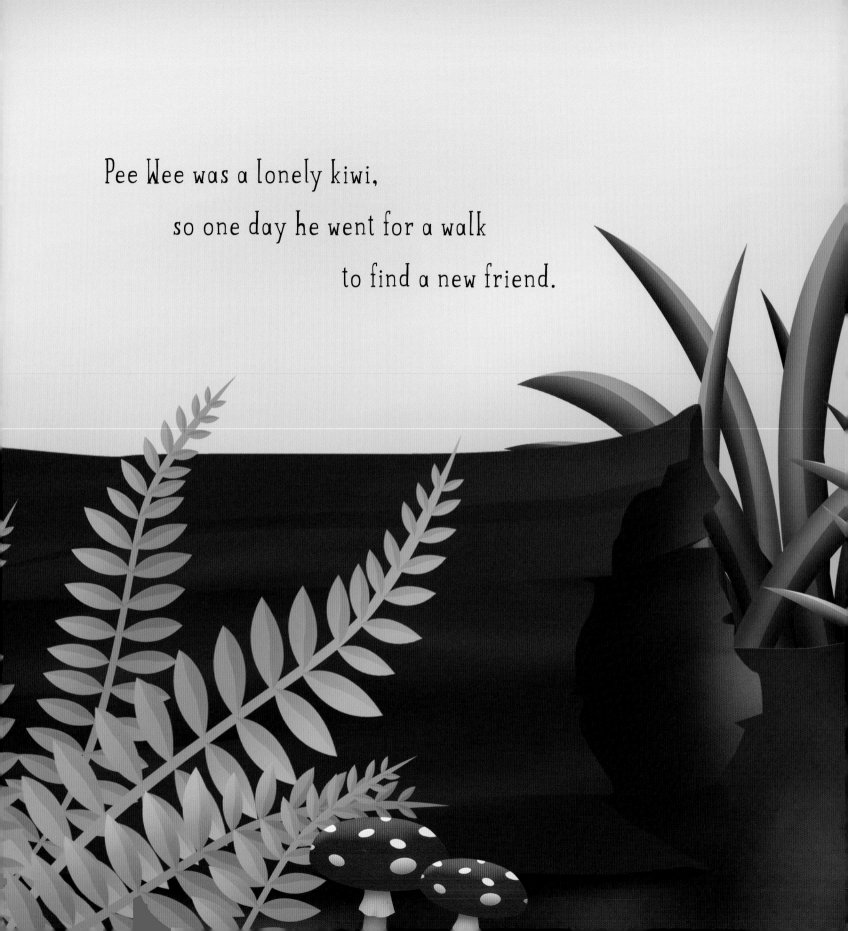

He walked over the hills
and through the trees,
all the way to the deep blue sea,

where he found ...

Bluely the penguin.

'Will you be my friend?' said Pee Wee the kiwi.

Bluely the penguin wanted to play.
Not on land, just in the waves.

But Pee Wee the kiwi couldn't swim.
The cold blue water put his head in a spin!

So Pee Wee the kiwi continued to walk ...

around the shore, over the rocks,

all the way to the mountain-tops,

where he found ...

Leah the kea.

'Will you be my friend?'

said Pee Wee the kiwi.

But Leah the kea was up to no good,

pulling a car aerial right off the hood!

Pee Wee the kiwi was a good little boy.

He wanted some friends to play with his toys.

So Pee Wee the kiwi continued to walk,

down the slopes, through the snow,

all the way to the valley below,

where he found ...

Stewie the tui!

'Will you be my friend?'
said Pee Wee the kiwi.

Stewie the tui sang a song in the trees.
A beautiful melody in
the gentle breeze.

Pee Wee the kiwi tried to join in,
but his beak was too long, and his voice too thin.
Stewie the tui was not impressed.
He flew far away, up to his nest.

So Pee Wee the kiwi continued to walk.

He walked around a lake, and through a rain shower,

all the way to a field full of flowers,

where he met ...

Thomas the thrush.

'Will you be my friend?'
said Pee Wee the kiwi.

Thomas the thrush was in a big rush,

and cried, 'You can come if you like, but don't run out of puff!'

But Thomas was too fast and the path was too rough.

Pee Wee the kiwi just couldn't keep up.

His little legs said, 'Enough is enough!',

making poor little Pee Wee fall to his butt.

So Pee Wee the kiwi continued to walk.

He walked down to the river,

home into the trees,

feeling tired, sad and not very pleased.

When, suddenly, along came ...

Noah the baby moa.

Noah the moa noticed Pee Wee looking ever so down,
with no one to talk to and wearing a very large frown.

'What's wrong, little one?' said Noah the moa.

'Well,' said Pee Wee, 'I can't swim, I can't fly, I can't sing in the sky. I don't have any friends, but I just don't know why ...'

'Well, I think you'd make a great friend,'
said Noah the baby moa.
'You are friendly and fun,
you can laugh, you can run,
but most of all you are a kind little kiwi.
How about you come with me?
We'll go and explore and have fun, you'll see.'

'I'd love to!', said Pee Wee the kiwi,

and off they went to play all day.

KIWI FACTS

The kiwi is a flightless bird native to New Zealand.

The kiwi is shy and usually nocturnal.

At around the size of a chicken, the kiwi is by far the smallest living flightless bird.

The kiwi eats seeds, grubs and many varieties of worms.

The kiwi has a highly developed sense of smell, which is unusual in a bird.

The kiwi lays the largest egg in relation to its body size of any species of bird in the world.

There are five recognised species of kiwi: the great spotted kiwi, little spotted kiwi, Okarito brown kiwi, Southern brown kiwi and the North Island brown kiwi, two of which are currently vulnerable, one endangered, and one critically endangered.